Ladybird  Readers

Nicky and Poppy

C334139295

Notes to teachers, parents, and carers

The *Ladybird Readers* Starter Level gently introduces children to the phonics approach to reading, by covering familiar themes that young readers will have studied (for example, colors, animals, and family).

Phonics focuses on how the individual sounds of letters are blended together to sound out a word. For example, /c/ /a/ /t/ when put together sound out the word **cat**.

The Starter Level is divided into two sub-level sections:
• **A** looks at simple words, such as **ant**, **dog**, and **red**.
• **B** explores trickier sound–letter combinations, such as the /**igh**/ sound in **night** and **fright**.

This book looks at the theme of **favorite food** and focuses on these sounds and letters:

p y qu n c h ng

There are some activities to do in this book. They will help children practice these skills:

 Spelling and writing    Speaking    Reading

LADYBIRD BOOKS

UK | USA | Canada | Ireland | Australia
India | New Zealand | South Africa

Ladybird Books is part of the Penguin Random House group of companies
whose addresses can be found at global.penguinrandomhouse.com.
www.penguin.co.uk   www.puffin.co.uk   www.ladybird.co.uk

Penguin
Random House
UK

First published 2017
001

Printed in China
A CIP catalogue record for this book is available from the British Library

ISBN: 978–0–241–29912–8

All correspondence to:
Ladybird Books
Penguin Random House Children's
80 Strand, London WC2R 0RL

MIX
Paper from
responsible sources
FSC® C018179

Ladybird Readers

Nicky and Poppy

Look at the story

Series Editor: Sorrel Pitts
Story by Coleen Degnan-Veness
Illustrated by Chris Jevons

Picture words

Nicky

Poppy

king

queen

Aa Bb Cc Dd Ee Ff Gg Hh Ii Jj Kk Ll Mm

pink

turnip

happy

not happy

behind

donkey

leek

eat

quiet

Use these words to help you with the activity on page 16.

Nicky happy pink turnip

Poppy

leek

king

queen

behind

donkey

quiet

not happy

turnip

leek

eat   happy

Activity

1 **Write the letters. Say the words.**

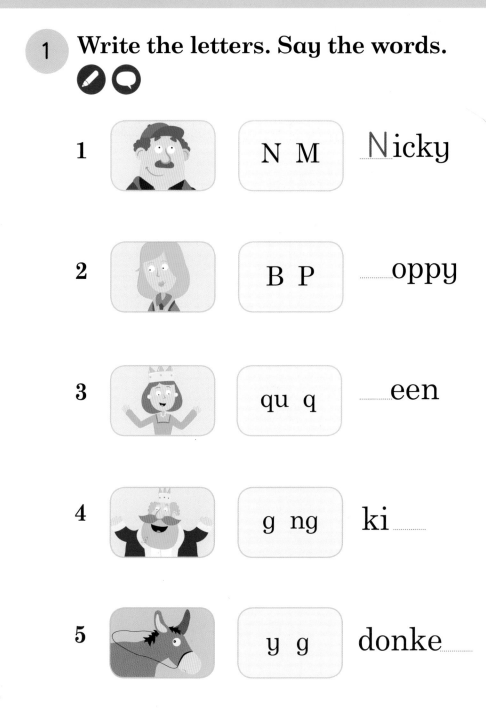

1   N M   Nicky

2   B P   ......oppy

3   qu q   ......een

4   g ng   ki......

5   y g   donke......

Nicky and Poppy

Read the story

Nicky is happy. He has got lots of pink turnips.

Poppy has got lots of leeks.

19

One pink turnip is very big.

Poppy has got a big leek.

Nicky is behind Poppy and her donkey.

23

The king and queen are quiet.

This is for the king.

This is for the queen.

The king and queen are
not happy. Nicky and
Poppy are quiet.

The king and queen are happy.

Activities

2   Look. Say the words. Match.

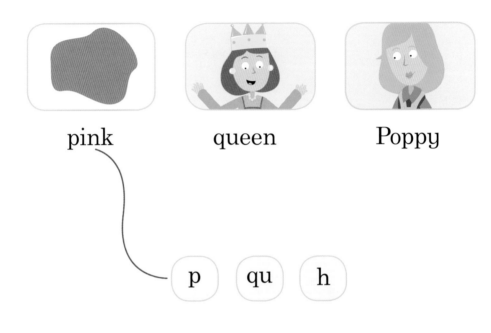

pink   queen   Poppy

p   qu   h

quiet

happy

3 **Look. Say the words.**
Put a ✓ **or a** ✗ **in the boxes.**

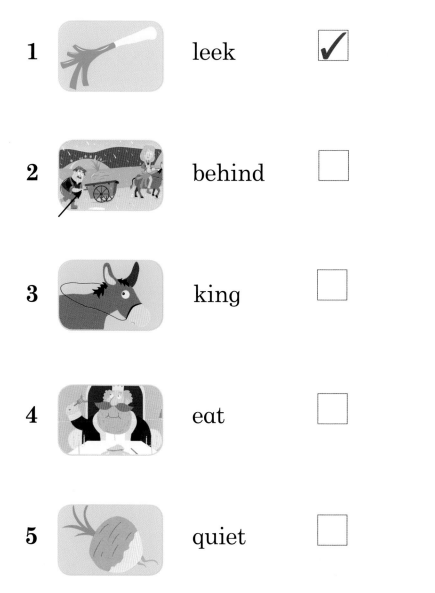

1   leek   ✓

2   behind   ☐

3   king   ☐

4   eat   ☐

5   quiet   ☐

4 Look. Say the sounds.
Write the letters.

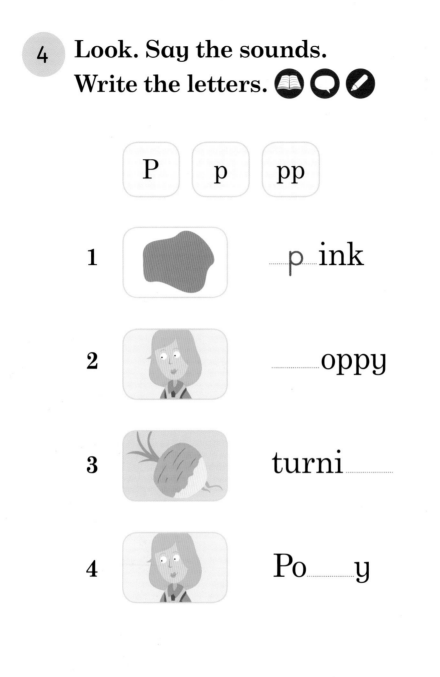

P	p	pp

1 p ink

2 _____oppy

3 turni_____

4 Po_____y

5 Read the words. Color in pink the words with the sound *n*. Find all the words.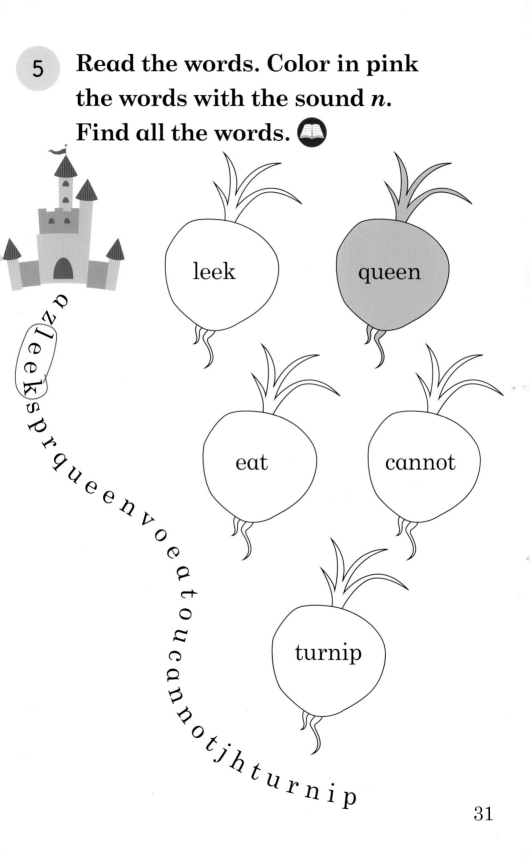

leek

queen

eat

cannot

turnip

azleeksprqueenvoeatoucannotjhturnip

Starter Level A and B

The Zoo
978–0–241–28346–2 ☐

Dom Dog and his Boat
978–0–241–28340–0 ☐

Ted in Bed
978–0–241–28342–4 ☐

The Fun Run
978–0–241–28343–1 ☐

Nicky and Poppy
978–0–241–29912–8 ☐

Doctor Panda
978–0–241–28339–4 ☐

Farmer Carl
978–0–241–28341–7 ☐

The Old Boat
978–0–241–28345–5 ☐

Brother Blue
978–0–241–28338–7 ☐

In the Mud
978–0–241–29913–5 ☐

The Big Fish
978–0–241–29915–9 ☐

Gus is Hot!
978–0–241–29914–2 ☐